Shallow Grave

Alex Van Tol

orca soundings

ORCA BOOK PUBLISHERS

Library and Archives Canada Cataloguing in Publication

Van Tol, Alex
Shallow grave / Alex Van Tol.
(Orca soundings)

Issued also in electronic formats.
ISBN 978-1-4598-0203-2 (BOUND).--ISBN 978-1-4598-0202-5 (PBK.)

I. Title. II. Series: Orca soundings
PS8643.A63S43 2012   jc813'.6   C2012-902577-1

First published in the United States, 2012
Library of Congress Control Number: 2012938213

Summary: Elliot and Shannon call forth a restless spirit when they are forced to
clean up an old boathouse as punishment for a school prank gone wrong.

Orca Book Publishers is dedicated to preserving the environment and has printed
this book on paper certified by the Forest Stewardship Council®.

Orca Book Publishers gratefully acknowledges the support for its publishing
programs provided by the following agencies: the Government of Canada
through the Canada Book Fund and the Canada Council for the Arts,
and the Province of British Columbia through the BC Arts Council
and the Book Publishing Tax Credit.

Cover photography by Dreamstime.com

ORCA BOOK PUBLISHERS
PO Box 5626, Stn. B
Victoria, BC Canada
v8R 6s4

ORCA BOOK PUBLISHERS
PO Box 468
Custer, WA USA
98240-0468

www.orcabook.com
Printed and bound in Canada.

15 14 13 12 • 4 3 2 1

For Mrs. Finch.
Your presence makes our lives
interesting.

You can check out any time you like,
but you can never leave.

—The Eagles,
"Hotel California," 1976

Chapter One

"This is awesome," I say. "Hard-core manual labor is exactly how I planned to spend my Friday after school."

With a loser goth weirdo in tow, I think. But I don't say that part.

"Well, it's not like I want to be cleaning up the boathouse either," Shannon shoots back. She claps her mittened hands together as we walk along the gravel road leading away from the school.

I grunt. Who wears mitts anyway? What is she, five?

I wonder if her palms are pierced too, or if it's just her cheek, nose, eyebrow, lip and tongue. And god knows what else.

I shudder at the thought.

"And anyway, I wouldn't exactly call it hard-core manual labor," she continues.

"So sorting through piles of old life jackets and busted paddles sounds like fun to you?"

She shakes her head. "Not fun. But not hard-core either. Hard-core is hiding the principal's Smart Car in the woods."

"No, that's what they call stupid," I say. The late October wind sneaks under the bottom of my hoodie and around my collar, making me shiver.

"It wasn't stupid. At least, it wouldn't have been if those idiots hadn't rolled it onto my foot. It would've been funny."

"Funny for you, maybe," I say. "Not so much fun for Mr. Harrison. And not funny for me. You should think twice before pulling dumb pranks that get innocent bystanders in trouble."

I can feel Shannon looking at me, but I don't return her gaze.

"Holy," she laughs. "Ease down there, Mr. Perfect. I already said I was sorry you got caught up in it. It's not like I planned for them to roll the car onto my foot. And anyway, I never asked you to come crashing through the bushes to save me, scholar boy."

"Scholar boy?"

Shannon ignores me. "You were in the wrong place at the wrong time," she says. "And you got in trouble. What's the big deal?"

I look at her in disbelief. "Ever heard the term 'miscarriage of justice'?"

She shrugs. "Life's unfair," she says. Then she gives me a sly smile. "Must be a hard pill to swallow for a rule follower like yourself."

"Since when is following rules a bad thing? Just because they're rules?"

"Depends on your reasons for following," she says. "I think you're one of those people who does what they're told because they've been brainwashed by the establishment."

I stop. "Excuse me?" I'm almost certain I didn't ask to have my character assaulted. Especially by a freak with purple hair and multiple puncture wounds whose crime I'm about to serve time for.

Besides. She doesn't even know me.

"Never mind." Shannon waves a hand dismissively. She keeps walking.

I don't move.

She turns and looks at me, then sighs. "I apologize, okay? For the millionth time." Her ultrawhite face and red lipstick look stark against the flat gray sky. She's dressed in a long black coat. A thick gray scarf winds around her neck. Docs on her feet. Those ugly boots are the only thing that saved her foot. She walked away instead of crawling.

Maybe I should've let her crawl.

"Honestly, Elliot," she says, "you're making a huge deal out of this. All we have to do is clean up the boathouse."

"Yeah, and who's going to clean up my record?" I ask. "I just started at this school two months ago, and already I got a rap."

As soon as I say it, I wish I hadn't. She'll just chalk it up to me wanting to impress the authorities. I try a different tack.

"Besides, why should those other jerks go free? They ran their little emo asses off when Harrison came. Beat a chickenshit retreat and left you stuck under the car." I shake my head.

"Who does that? They should be here cleaning up too."

"Don't worry about them," Shannon says. "Karma's watching. They'll get what they deserve somewhere down the line." She tucks a strand of purple behind her ear. "Besides, you should be glad. You collected lots of positive karmic points for trying to help." She grins. "Especially someone who obviously doesn't fit on your spectrum of...social acceptability."

I can't argue with that.

"How could I not stop and help?" I say. "You were screaming like someone was tearing your heart out of your chest."

"My hero, Elliot the A-student jock superstar." She clasps her hands under her chin and flutters her eyelashes.

Girl's got a chip on her shoulder a mile wide.

I bite my tongue. Take a deep breath and release it very, very slowly. I count to ten, like that buck-toothed psychiatrist taught me how to do back when my parents split and I was beating the crap out of everything within arm's reach.

This could be a long afternoon.

Chapter Two

If it weren't for this stupid situation,
Shannon and I would never have had
any reason to cross paths. We don't run
with the same crowds. Not that I have
such an established crowd after only
seven weeks at Wildwood, but there are
some good people in it.

Smart people. People who work
hard. People who want to do well

in school so they can do well in the world.

I'm not so sure I could say the same about her crowd.

In the last seven days since Mr. Harrison walked in on us in the bushes, I've learned how different Shannon and I are as people. "Like chalk and cheese," my grandmother would say.

I swim for the national team. Shannon writes mouthy articles for the school newspaper.

I work hard and apply myself so my mom's not wasting her money sending me to a school like this. Shannon breaks the rules no matter who's paying.

I like to look respectable and approachable. Shannon likes to shock people.

I am black. Shannon is white.

End of story.

When I pulled in last Friday morning after my doctor's appointment—a long needle in my foot for another plantar wart from a dirty pool deck—I'd seen the principal, Mr. Harrison, leaving the building. My mom wanted me to ask him about missing some school. There was a big tri-state meet in November, and I was going to have to miss a couple of days on either side of the weekend. This seemed to be as good an opportunity as any to speak with him.

I parked and grabbed my bag.

Once I was out of the car, though, I couldn't exactly ignore the shrieks coming from the bushes at the edge of the parking lot.

I forgot about talking to Mr. Harrison and went over to investigate.

Okay, I ran over with my heart in my throat. I thought someone was being assaulted.

One glance told me all I needed to know. There was this purple-haired girl with her foot stuck under the tire of one of those little Smart Cars. Swearing a blue streak. Two skinny weak types were yelling at each other. A third guy dressed head to toe in black was hissing at the girl to keep it down. Four or five other people were pelting down a forest trail, away from the scene.

Holy crap. They actually rolled a car into the bushes.

Purple Girl was shrieking. "Don't tell me to shut up, Ramone. Just get this goddamn thing off my foot!"

I cleared my throat. Heads whipped in my direction. They seemed shocked to see me. Like it never occurred to them that hysterical screams coming from the forest might attract attention.

"Uh," I said. "Is this Mr. Harrison's car? 'Cause he's on his way over." I nodded over my shoulder, toward the parking lot. "I just saw him leaving the school."

It wasn't going to take him long to notice that his car was gone. I'm sure he'd already heard the screams and was wondering what the hell was going on in the bushes.

The other guys all looked at each other. "Shit," said the Ramone guy. "Harrison."

I bent to brace my shoulder against the back of the car.

Purple Girl threw me a grateful look. "Thank god," she said. "Someone who has half a brain."

I didn't even know her name then.

"You guys going to help or what?" I asked, looking up.

It was like my words broke them out of their spell. They took off, leaving the girl and me behind. I had to push the Smart Car off her foot by myself.

Which wasn't that hard, really.

What was hard was getting treated like a criminal for trying to be a nice guy.

Mr. Harrison didn't care that I wasn't in on the plan. He's a dick like that, I discovered. All that matters is his own view of things. Smash through bushes. See two kids standing next to car. Car in wrong spot. One kid looks like he's maybe the wrong color. Must punish. Hard. I guess it didn't help that I'm new this year and he doesn't know me. He had his own conclusions to jump to.

I can see why you'd want to hide his car. The guy's a jerk.

That was a week ago. And now here we are.

Shannon didn't rat out the other nerds who were in on the prank, even though she had every right. I guess that's respectable in some circles.

But it doesn't make me any less pissed off.

Chapter Three

The faded red boathouse looms up in front of us, eerie in the dying daylight. A padlock hangs from the ring on the door.

Low-grade anger simmers in my gut as my cold fingers fumble with the keys. Mr. Harrison handed them to me with a little sneer when I reported to the office after school today.

"Let's see if you're as good at cleaning as you are at messing with private property, Owens."

I didn't trust myself to try and explain it to him. Again.

I just took the keys, looked him in the eye and gave him a nod. Let him figure out in time how mistaken he's been.

I select a key that looks like it'll fit the big padlock. But before I can slide it in, the shackle swings open. Not even locked.

I pocket the key and pull the door open.

That old-wooden-building smell hits me.

"Watch your step," I say over my shoulder. The boathouse is raised on concrete blocks. I point to the space separating the floor from the ground so Shannon doesn't trip on her way in. I don't want to have to carry her out of here if she falls and breaks something.

"Lights?" Shannon asks. She's standing beside me in the doorway.

I fumble around for a switch. "I don't think there are any," I say.

"That's weird," she says. Our eyes adjust to the darkness. "It's creepy in here."

"Nah," I say. But I don't mean it. I just want to disagree with her, even though she's right. The place is creepy as hell.

What's left of the daylight streams in through a high window. I set the heavy padlock down on a shelf. Something scuttles across the roof. Our heads turn toward the sound.

"Squirrels?" Shannon asks.

"Maybe. Or rats."

"Rats?" Her voice comes out small.

I nod. "They've probably made nests in the eaves."

She shivers. I wouldn't have thought a punk like her could be nervous. She seems so sure of herself.

Maybe she's afraid of nature. Sometimes people like that are. It's easier to feel rebellious in the city. You can fool yourself into thinking you're strong when you're surrounded by concrete and skyscrapers.

I decide to ask her what I've been wondering. "What did Harrison do, anyway, that made you guys want to take off with his car?"

She shoots me a look. "He's a prick. You've seen that for yourself."

That's the truth.

"And he muzzles free speech. It sucks." Her voice is hard. "I get it all the time with the newspaper. The guy doesn't know how to have any fun."

I nod. "He's having fun now, thinking about us cleaning out this dump on a Friday afternoon."

Shannon laughs. The sound surprises a smile out of me. I look away.

My eyes make out a glint of glass at the rear of the boathouse. I head toward the back, where a series of glass hurricane lamps line a shelf.

Shannon follows behind. "Oh goody!" She claps her hands, still in their mittens. "We can work by candlelight."

Oh goody.

We feel around on the shelf beside the lanterns.

"Hah?" Shannon holds up a box of Redbird wooden matches. "Am I good or what?"

A dozen smart comebacks march through my mind, but I say nothing.

I pick up one of the lanterns and tip it. Kerosene splashes up the inside wall of the glass reservoir at the bottom. Lots of fuel. I take the chimney off the top and roll the wick down to wet it.

Shannon lights a match and holds it to the wick. She's wearing that weird nail polish that looks all smashed, like her nails have been hit with a hammer. Black, of course.

We light three more lanterns, placing them in different spots in the old building.

As I place the last one, I catch sight of the overhead light. It's a naked bulb in the center of the ceiling. A thin cord of string hangs down a few inches. I missed it in the dark, thinking the switch would be on the wall. But, of course, the boathouse is old and so is the wiring.

I pull on the string. A dim light floods the interior.

Shannon looks up. "Ah!" she exclaims, then laughs again. "All that trouble!" Then she looks around at the kerosene lanterns. "But I kind of like the lamps too. Let's leave them burning."

"Whatever turns your crank," I say. Even with the light from the lanterns and overhead bulb, the place is dark.

"Will you write me a poem by the firelight, oh handsome one?" she teases. I guess she's forgotten to be angry with me for being a rule follower.

Or maybe it was only me who was angry.

"I'm an athlete," I say. "Not one of your fairy-art friends." The words come out harsher than I had meant. But whatever.

Shannon blinks.

God, let's just get this job over with.

Behind us, the door bangs against the frame. I jump, and Shannon lets out a little squeak. We look at each other. She laughs nervously.

I prop the door open with a big brick, and we look around.

It smells musty in here, like dust and old damp things. Rope. Mildew. Wooden things. Boatish things. Our eyes travel the room, taking in the surroundings. There's stuff everywhere—in piles, in boxes, on shelves, on the floor.

Shannon puts words to my thoughts. "This is going to take us awhile."

Chapter Four

"So what's the plan of attack?" Shannon slings her bag into a corner. Two hard-cover books slide out onto the floor. A science text and some big silver book. A tube of lip stuff clatters out and comes to rest against the spine of the silver book. Two metal bracelets roll away under a shelf. Shannon sighs but doesn't move to pick stuff up.

I turn my head a bit so I can read the writing on the silver book. *Wildwood Composite 2011–2012*. The new yearbook.

I look up to see Shannon standing with her hands on her hips, all business like. I sigh. "We go through everything," I say. "Keep the things that still work. Paddles, PFDS, sprayskirts. Toss stuff that's old or busted."

"Like this?" Shannon holds up a broken plastic bucket.

"Like that."

She chucks it toward the door. "We can make a garbage pile over there," she says. "Then when we're done, we can shove it all into bags and carry it down to the Dumpsters."

I move toward a rack of PFDS. "Nice to know you got it all worked out," I say.

She misses my dart, responding with a cheery, "You're in good hands!"

I roll my eyes and shake out a plastic bag. I put the broken bucket inside it and set the bag down by the door. Then I get to work.

I count and organize the life jackets. Shannon sits on the floor behind me, rifling through a bin of maps, rope and colored pinnies.

"So do you paddle?" she asks, tossing a roll of tape onto a pile.

"No, I swim," I say.

"I know you swim, Elliot," she says. "You're on the national team." I glance over at her. She throws me a sweet smile.

I study her for a moment, trying to decide whether she's making fun of me.

"I'd like to learn how," she says.

"To swim?" I ask.

She laughs and shakes her head. "I know how to swim," she says. "I mean it might be cool to learn how to paddle."

This surprises me. "Yeah?" She doesn't exactly strike me as the outdoorsy type. I wonder what she looks like without all that makeup on.

She nods. "We used to do a lot of camping when I was little."

I can't see it. But I don't say it.

Shannon sighs and holds up a section of rope. "This knot's going to take me all night," she says.

I grunt and look down at the one I'm trying to undo. I wish she'd stop talking. I just want to get this job done. She's not exactly my pick of conversation partners.

"What would you be doing otherwise?" Shannon asks. "If you weren't cleaning up a boathouse?"

There's no way this girl can work quietly. She's a total motormouth. I'm going to have to talk.

"On a Friday night?" I say. "Probably playing Rock Band or watching movies at someone's house."

"After you do the vacuuming and finish all your homework?"

"Not exactly," I say. "We have a cleaning lady who comes in to do the vacuuming."

I look up. Shannon's staring at me, her thoughts right there on her face. Spoiled rich kid. The world handed to him on a platter.

But that's just the way it seems to her. It's not how things really are.

No one's life is really what you think it is. Not from the outside.

As she stares, I feel my ears grow hot. "You got the homework part right though," I say.

The tension eases a little.

I look back at the knot. "And I have to clean my room too. I'm actually not allowed out until it's done."

Shannon laughs then. Glad, I guess, to think I have normal problems like other people. "At least then you get it out of the way," she says.

I shrug. "I guess. I spend most of the weekend swimming, so I kind of have to. I'm way too tired by Sunday night." I tug at the knot with my teeth. Damn, this thing's tight. "Your Friday nights?"

She thinks for a minute. "Probably cleaning up my mother's mess before I take off. I usually crash with friends on weekends."

I look up. "You clean up your mom's mess? That's a switch. Don't most mothers complain that their kids make the messes?"

"I wouldn't know," Shannon says. "Mine's a depressed alcoholic who spends her days lying on the sofa eating Chunky Monkey and watching reality TV."

I lower the rope and look at her. "Wow."

Her voice is light, but she keeps her eyes down. "Yeah. Well, sometimes she switches to Chubby Hubby, though, so it's not all bad." She laughs.

"I'm sorry."

"About the ice cream?" She sighs. "I know. It's a problem."

"No, I mean, about…"

Shannon lifts a shoulder. "No biggie. It is what it is."

But I'm sure she wishes it wasn't.

"Where's your dad?" I'm always curious about other people's parents, since one of mine pretty much up and disappeared.

"Saudi Arabia," she says.

Oh. One of those families. I've heard things get messed up when your parents travel overseas for work. I think about what Shannon's home life must look like. I can't imagine my mother even lying on the sofa, let alone eating ice cream in front of the TV. I don't even think I've ever seen her lie down. She doesn't know how to stop moving.

"Ha!" Shannon holds up the length of nylon she's been working on. "Behold the knot-free rope!"

"Nice," I say. I'm relieved to change the subject. It sounds like a depressing life. I hold the PFD out toward her. "Here. Try this one. I'm not having any luck."

"Not a chance," she says. "I've had enough knots for the time being." She stands and stretches. "What about these bins here, on the shelves?"

"Check them all," I say.

"Most of this stuff is in pretty good shape, actually," she says, pulling back a couple of tops and peering inside. "It's just not very well organized. I think once we get it all into the right places, we'll be done."

"Maybe it won't take us the whole night, after all," I say. As I say the words, the knot in the cord finally loosens.

"Hey," Shannon says. Her voice is muffled. "What's this?"

I look over. Shannon's leaning forward, her upper body buried deep inside a blue bin. She's standing on her tiptoes, reaching. She'd have nice legs if she didn't go around covering them up with that ugly fishnet crap.

That's a pretty short skirt. I wonder if she really might have a tattoo on her bum.

I lean forward a little to see if I can influence the view.

Suddenly she straightens and her skirt drops back down. I look down and get busy with pulling the final loops out of the cord. I feel a flush creeping up. I'm glad she can't tell.

"Check it out," she says. I glance up as casually as I can. A silver chain dangles from her fingers. In the center hangs a little pendant.

"A necklace."

"A necklace," she agrees. "Well, half a necklace. Have you ever seen these before?" She comes closer and squats down to show me. "It's one of those friendship necklaces. This is one half."

I look at the pendant resting on Shannon's fingers. It says BEST in fancy silver lettering.

"One friend gets the best and the other one gets the friends," Shannon continues. "Sometimes they even fit together, like pieces of a puzzle." She runs the chain through her fingers. I wonder if she's thinking about stealing it.

"I wonder who this belonged to," she says. Her eyes are on the pendant.

"No clue," I say. I finish untwisting the cord. "Anything else weird in that box?" I stand and hang the PFD with the others.

Shannon goes back to the box and bends over to peer inside.

Damn. Why'd I stand up?

"I don't think so," she says, moving a few things around. "There's mostly just a bunch of rope." She holds up a coil of medium rope, like you'd use for tying up canoes.

"Must've just fallen off whoever was wearing it." I start stacking folded tarps on a low shelf.

"I bet the other friend was sad," says Shannon.

"Or mad," I offer.

Shannon grins. "Or secretly relieved."

The door bangs shut, making me jump. "What the—?"

Shannon drops the necklace and screams.

Which scares the pants off me.

"Jesus!" I yell. "Don't freak out like that!"

Shannon's staring at the door, her eyes huge and her hands pressed against her chest.

"It's just the door," I say. "Relax."

"Yeah, but…"

"But nothing, man. You just about gave me a coronary." My heart's beating a frenzied rhythm somewhere around my molars. I bend over and pick up the tarp I dropped when she screamed.

"But…" Shannon says. She tears her eyes away from the door and looks at me. "You propped it open, Elliot."

She looks back at the door. "With a cinderblock."

Chapter Five

It wasn't a cinderblock though. Not really. Just a big brick. Big enough to have stood up to the wind, I thought, but apparently not.

I guess one strong gust was all it took to just...tip it over.

It's freezing outside anyway, and there's not much daylight left, so I close the door all the way. There's a little hook-and-eye clasp on the inside. I drop the hook into the eye.

"There. No more banging," I say. "We are locked in."

I'm feeling a bit looser after that scare. And after our conversation. I might be stuck in a boathouse with a dorky punk chick, but it's actually more fun than…well, than cleaning my room and doing homework.

"I'm not so sure that's such a good thing," Shannon says. She throws me a sidelong glance.

"What, being locked in?" I ask. "Why? You afraid of the boogeyman?"

"There's no such thing," she says.

I open my mouth, but before I can say anything, my stomach growls. Loudly.

Shannon laughs.

"So maybe there's no boogeyman," I say. "There is, however, such a thing as hunger."

I pull out my phone and glance at it. 4:09. "You hungry?"

"I could eat," she says. "I have pita and hummus from my lunch. Enough for two."

"Pita and hummus," I scoff. "How about Texas donuts?"

Shannon's mouth drops open. "You have Texas donuts?"

I nod. "Fresh from the fundraiser," I say. "People who ordered but never picked up." I realize how nerdy that must make me sound, especially to her. Fundraisers. Her kind don't exactly go in for that.

More like welfare.

As soon as I think it, the thought makes me ashamed. Until today, I'd never met anyone whose home life was like Shannon's.

If you can even call it a home life.

In fact, until today, I'd never really even talked to someone like Shannon. So who the hell am I to judge?

"Texas donuts," Shannon is saying in a dreamy voice. "Act of god? Or pure karma?"

She's so bizarre.

I pull a cardboard sleeve from my bag and flip it open to reveal two gigantic donuts. They're squashed, and the cheap chocolate icing is sliding off the top, but we dig in like two starving animals.

Shannon looks around as she chews. "There's something weird in here."

"Like what? Did you find a hair?"

"No," she laughs.

She laughs a lot, but somehow the sound catches me by surprise every time.

"Not in the donut," she says. "In the boathouse."

"Think so?" I ask. I take another bite and look around. "Like?"

"I don't know. Something."

"Well, there's the rats," I say.

"No, no, more like…something else. A presence."

"Maybe it's a ghost," I say. "O-o-o-o."

Shannon raises one perfect, dark eyebrow and fixes me with a stare. "Maybe it is."

My turn to laugh. "Oh, come on. Do you actually believe in stuff like that?"

She shrugs. "Who's to say spirits don't exist?"

I roll my eyes. "Oh my god. So do you believe in UFOS too?" Come to think of it, she seems like the type to believe in anything.

She gives a little half smile. "Maybe." She looks around the boathouse. I can see her forming an idea. When she turns back to me, her eyes are shining.

This can't be good.

"I have an idea," she says.

Aaaaand there it is.

I speak slowly, imagining my words as a fine mist of wisdom heavy enough to weigh down her impulsivity.

"Your ideas have been known to get people into trouble," I say.

"I think we should make a Ouija board," she says.

She's not feeling the mist.

"I think we should finish our work and go home."

"No, no," she says. "I want to see if there's something in here."

I don't like the way this is headed.

"Those Ouija board things are bunk," I say. "They don't even work."

I have no idea if this is true. I'm grasping at straws here.

"Oh, they work all right," she says. "I've done it before. It's freaky. The way the thing moves around all by itself and everything."

I look at her. She looks like a kid who's just been told she's leaving for Disneyland tomorrow.

There's no way I'm going to be able to talk her out of this.

"Are you a glutton for punishment or something?" I say. "Weren't you just screaming in abject terror not five minutes ago because the door slammed?"

She laughs. "It wasn't *abject*. It just surprised me, is all." She looks around. "But seriously, what if there is something here?" She takes another bite of donut and brushes a couple of crumbs from her lap.

I'm not sure what to think. Maybe she's one of those people who likes to feel bad things. Like when your braces get tightened and your whole jaw aches, but you still clench your teeth because you get off on the pain.

Okay, I'll admit I've done that.

Maybe I should just loosen up a bit, I think. Maybe it's not that big a deal. It's not like I've got any fantastic plans for later tonight anyway.

Besides, Ouija's just a party game. They sell it in boxes at Toys "R" Us, for god's sake. How real can it possibly be?

Chapter Six

Shannon finishes the rest of her donut. She crumples the paper towel and tosses it toward the door, where our garbage pile is growing.

Her tongue piercing flashes as she licks her fingers. I look away.

When I look back, she's sitting cross-legged, staring expectantly at me.

"What?" I ask. Maybe she saw me

staring at her tongue.

"You ready?"

I sigh. "I see you don't know how to take no for an answer," I say.

"No?" she says. She cocks her head and furrows her brows in mock confusion. "What's that?"

I fight a smile. "Fine. I'm down," I say. "Let's just do it and get out of here."

Shannon's face lights up, and she leans toward me. For a panicky second, I think she's going to kiss me and I try to think of what to do. Look away? Lean backward? Kiss her back? What do I do about the tongue thing?

But she doesn't kiss me. She puts both her hands on my knees and gives them a little squeeze.

I feel pretty dumb.

And a little disappointed.

Shannon grins and scrambles to her feet. "This is going to be so much fun!" she says.

"There's only one problem," I say.

"What's that?"

"We don't have a Ouija board."

Ha. See what she says to that.

She points to a nearby bin. "I saw some old chalkboards in here," she says. "We'll use the back of one of those."

"You can't do that," I say. "Those don't belong to us."

Shannon stares at me. "You can't be serious," she says.

"I'm totally serious." I'm not, really, but she already thinks I'm such a Goody Two-shoes. Maybe she'll agree with me and just forget about the whole idea.

"Then what else are we supposed to use?" she demands.

I shrug and look around. I point to the yearbook on the floor.

Her eyes follow my finger. "What? No way." She sounds shocked, like I've just suggested she take all her clothes off and dance naked at the next assembly. "I just bought that today. That cost me fifty bucks! I'm not going to go marking it up with a Sharpie."

The irony kills me. "Oh, so you're okay with making a mess of other people's stuff, but not your own?"

She opens her mouth, then closes it again. She raises her chin and looks at me.

"We'll use chalk." Her eyes dare me to argue.

There's no winning.

She reaches into the bin. Her hand pops back out holding up a flat board about the size of a breakfast tray.

"This," she says, handing it to me, "is perfect."

"Wow," I say, turning the board around in my hands. "It's so old school. How does it work?"

"No idea. I can't find the power button."

I laugh. I try not to notice her eyes lighting up.

"So you can actually just…make a Ouija board?" I say. "I thought you had to buy them."

"They're actually more effective when they're made by hand," Shannon says. "More powerful."

"Are we going for powerful?"

She doesn't answer. Just motions for me to put the board down on the floor. She turns back to the bin and digs around until she comes up with a short stick of chalk.

"You've done this before?" I ask. She kneels on the floor beside me. I watch as she bends her head and writes YES in the top left corner.

"Couple times," she says. She writes NO in the top right, then drops down a line and starts writing the letters of the alphabet.

"What's it like?"

Shannon's concentrating on making her letters neat and evenly spaced. She touches her tongue to her upper lip as she works. I think about that metal barbell again.

She finishes the first row, A through K, and sits up straight. "It's cool," she says. "But it can be kind of scary too. You have to stay in control of the board at all times. You can't just take your hands off, or walk away. There's rules."

"Yeah, but you're no good at following rules," I say.

"Shut up!" She boots me in the ankle. "I know how to follow rules. I just choose which ones are important. And which ones aren't." She gives me a meaningful look.

Her earlier jab hangs between us, unspoken. I let it.

"Why's it so important to keep your hands on the board?" I ask. "Do things get out of control if you don't?"

She starts on the second row. The letters follow a slight curve, like a rainbow.

"Don't know. I've never taken my hands off," she says. Her hand moves smoothly as she writes. P. Q. R. S. She's careful not to smudge the other letters as she works.

"You ever had weird things happen while you're doing it?" I've heard the stories people tell. The one where people were doing Ouija and something fell on the floor upstairs. When they went to investigate, they found that a Bible had fallen off a shelf.

I'd also heard the story about the two long claw marks found on the back of a basement door.

And the two trees that fell side by side at the same time, smashing a garage to pieces. Strong trees. No wind.

All different stories. I'd always dismissed them as crap.

But now, sitting in the gloom of an old boarded-up boathouse with the cold seeping through the cracks in the floor, I'm not so sure.

Shannon finishes the second row and straightens. "Yeah, I've had freaky things happen," she says, studying the board. "One time the spirit I was talking with wouldn't say goodbye."

"So? What's the big deal with saying goodbye?"

"Well, when you use a Ouija board, you're opening a portal to the spirit world," Shannon replies. She bends forward to start on the final few letters. "Maybe you get a friendly one, and maybe you don't. It's hard to tell. But friendly or not, you still have to say goodbye."

"Yeah, but can't you just take your hands off the board? Break the connection or something?"

She shakes her head. "No, because remember? Then you're giving up control.

Leaving the portal open. And if you don't close out your session with an actual goodbye that the board consents to, you can't close the portal." She writes the digits one through zero near the bottom of the board.

I snort. "What, so you leave open the door to hell?"

Shannon blows the chalk dust away, then glances up at me. "You might."

I feel a chill.

"Almost done," she says.

Then I think of something. "Won't the chalk wipe off?" I ask.

She answers without looking up. "Better hope not."

On the bottom left-hand side of the board, Shannon neatly letters HELLO.

On the right, she prints GOODBYE.

Chapter Seven

By the time the board's ready for action, I'm ready to pack it in. My feet are freezing, and my adrenal glands are pumping out enough juice to fuel sixty thoroughbreds on a long-distance race.

"Okay," Shannon says. "We need to find something that will work as a planchette."

"A what?"

"The thing you put your fingers on. The thing that slides around the board." She looks around. "A lid would work."

I guess we're really going through with this.

"How about the cap to a bleach bottle? There's some homemade bailers over there," she says, nodding to a cardboard box in the corner. "They've all got caps on the bottom."

I go and retrieve one of the bailers. I unscrew the white lid from the plastic neck and hand it to Shannon. She places it on the board and motions for me to sit across from her. I do.

"Okay, so. Ground rules," she says.

I nod.

"First, no taking your hands off the cap."

"Or else we'll lose control and Satan will enter the room."

Shannon slaps at my arm. "Stop saying that!" But there's a smile in her eyes.

"Second, I'll ask the questions." She gives me a pointed look. "It's important to be respectful and polite."

I raise an eyebrow. "And you think that's a problem for me?"

"You're a smart-ass, Elliot. If I let you run this session, you'll get us both killed."

I sigh.

"And third, don't ever do it alone," she says. "Not that you'll be alone today. But if you ever do it again."

"Why can't you do it alone?"

"You should always have someone else there. You're trying to connect with a world we don't really understand, you know?" Shannon explains. "Back to that thing about staying in control."

I nod. An idea hits me. "Hey," I say, "can we talk to Kurt Cobain?"

"Oooh, that would be awesome!" she says. Then she shakes her head. "But it doesn't work like that. You can't call a specific person up from the dead.

That's more like what goes on in a séance. And those are seriously freaky."

"So we just talk to…random ghosts?" I say. "What's the point of that?"

Shannon leans across the board, eyes wide. "Because it's a trip, that's what!" She sits back and grins. "And who knows?" She looks around. "Maybe we'll be able to talk to whatever's here."

"If there even is something here," I say. My last word comes out high and thin. Is it me, or did a rush of cold air just sweep the back of my neck?

I glance at Shannon to see if she noticed my sudden falsetto, but she's getting herself settled on a PFD.

I must have imagined that. God, I'm freaking myself out over nothing.

The PFD's a good idea, actually. Put something between my skinny ass and this freezing cold floor. I reach for one and stuff it under me.

"Ready?" Shannon asks.

Alex Van Tol

I nod.

She pushes the bottle cap over to HELLO.

"Put your hands on," she instructs. "Just your fingertips, really lightly. You don't want to be pushing on the disc."

I place my fingertips on the cap, copying her.

"We'd like to ask a few questions," Shannon says. Her voice is loud. I glance at her, but she's talking to the board. My stomach tightens.

"Is there a spirit present?"

Nothing happens.

"We welcome your presence," she says. "We would like to speak with you. Would you like to speak with us?"

We sit, our fingertips almost touching across the top of the bottle cap. I study her nail polish.

Nothing happens.

This is lame.

52

Suddenly I feel incredibly stupid. What am I so worried about? I'm sitting with my fingers on the cap to an old bleach bottle, freaking out over talking to a bunch of letters that have been printed on an old chalkboard.

And—big surprise—the letters aren't talking back.

"Would you like to speak with us?" Shannon asks again.

Nothing. Our fingers quiver, moving the cap infinitesimally. Ideomotor movement. Just our smallest muscular movements affecting the placement of the lid. I've heard people say that's all Ouija is. Just a bunch of nervous movements being taken way too seriously by whoever's making them.

Shannon tries again. "Is there someone here, in this building? Are you familiar with this building?"

No response.

I take a deep breath and relax my shoulders.

"Looks like the spirits are asleep." I catch Shannon's eye and grin.

And then the cap moves.

Chapter Eight

I guess I really wasn't expecting it. Skipping and stuttering a bit, the cap slides on a diagonal. Across the board. Away from HELLO.

Toward YES.

I yank my hands away.

"Put your fingers back on!" Shannon barks.

I put them back. She flashes me a look. "You can't leave me alone on the board."

The cap stopped when I took my fingers off. It sits quietly now, paused between L and C.

I feel like an idiot.

But I also feel incredibly nervous.

Okay, fine. I'm afraid.

My fingertips feel hot where they touch the cap. Which is weird, because it's cold in here. Maybe I'm pressing too hard. I ease off a bit until they're just barely grazing the plastic. Still hot.

I consider telling Shannon I'm just not that into it, but that would make me look like a sissy. So I don't.

Shannon turns her attention back to the board. "I'll ask the question again," she says. "Are you familiar with this building?"

The cap stutters. My heart skips out a double beat and my ears whoosh with the sudden rush in my pulse. I force my fingers to stay put as the cap staggers toward the top of the board.

YES.

Shannon glances at me. "Were you ever inside this building?"

The cap inches to the other side of the board. *Scuff. Scuff-scuff.*

NO.

Somehow this makes me feel relieved.

"Were you a student at this school?"

The cap flies backward, sliding like a puck on ice. *Shhh.*

YES.

"Whoa," Shannon says. Her voice is shaky.

I can't help it. I jerk my fingers away again. "What the hell?" I whisper.

"Elliot!"

Like a robot, I put them back. My head feels light, like I'm only half here. Shannon glares at me.

She looks back at the board. "What's your name?"

Nothing.

"What is your name?" Shannon repeats, a little louder.

No movement.

My fingertips hurt. It's like I'm holding them against a heater. Those couple of seconds before your nerves realize they're being barbecued.

"Are you happy?"

What kind of question is that? What ghost is happy? Do happy ghosts haunt places?

I'm not surprised by the board's answer: NO.

"Great," I mutter.

Shannon scowls at me.

"Why are you here?"

Nothing.

"Too broad," Shannon says under her breath. She raises her voice a bit. "When did you die?"

The cap skids forward. A sudden tightness seizes the back of my brain, and my vision blurs. I want to tell Shannon to stop, but my tongue feels thick, like someone's stuffed a sock in my mouth.

The cap slides to a halt.

J

Slides away.

U

Slides again.

N

I have a vague notion that I'm leaning backward, my head turned away from the board.

Shannon's brow furrows. "J-U-N?" she asks. "Do you mean June? Did you die in June?"

Moving again.

YES.

I bite down on a little moan.

There's an invisible presence in here, and it's talking to us.

"You died in June," Shannon says. "Was it this past June?"

YES.

Shannon blinks. Licks her lips.

"Are you a girl?"

YES.

Shannon's eyes widen, and she takes a little breath. "Oh my god," she whispers. Then she looks at me. "I think I know who this is."

"What?" I mouth back. So now she actually knows this dead person we're talking to? Man, this is just too much for me.

"Were you ready to die?" Shannon asks.

The lid shoots toward the corner of the board.

NO.

A shiver starts somewhere in my core and works itself outward, leaving me cold. So cold. Like I've fallen through ice. But yet, my fingers are still burning. My stomach curls in on itself.

"What is your name?" Shannon asks.

The cap moves fast.

GOODBYE.

Shannon lets out a shaky breath. I can't pull my hands from the lid soon enough. I blow on my fingertips to cool them.

We sit, ghostly white and staring at each other.

Then the phone rings.

Chapter Nine

Shannon screams. She screams so loud, it drowns out my own scream. Then she grabs me and we scream together.

We stare at the phone. I don't remember taking it out of my pocket. But then, yes, I do. I checked the time before we ate the donuts.

The display clearly tells me it's my swim coach. Not hell calling. But I can't move to pick it up.

When the phone stops ringing, we stay like that, locked together, for a few seconds. Panting, we stare at the phone.

I'm the first to release. Shannon moves back to her side of the board, gathering her hair to one side of her neck. "Holy cats," she says. "That was intense."

"That's one way to describe it," I agree. If this wasn't happening to me, I'd be laughing. Because it's straight out of a horror movie.

Lucky for us, the scary part is behind us. We're not stupid like the idiots in the movies. The fools who open doors to strangers at nighttime or who follow the big bad crashing noises through the woods to see what's making them.

We're not stupid like that, because we're going to put the Ouija board back with the rest of the chalkboards and hang up our PFDS and then get the hell out of here. I'll talk Hatch and Mike into coming back with me on Sunday after practice. We'll bring a few of those big-ass bright camping lanterns and get this place cleaned up.

I gather up the cardboard and the paper towels and stuff them into the garbage bag by the door. Screw recycling. I'm getting out of here.

"Where are you going?" Shannon asks.

"Home," I say. "I've had enough fun for the next few years, I think."

Shannon laughs. "Pretty freaky, eh? I love it."

"I'm not feeling the love," I say. "I'm feeling like it's time to go."

"But I want to find out more," she protests. "We've only just begun. And I think I know who we're talking to."

"How? Who?" I ask. Then quickly I add, "Never mind. Tell me in the car.

I gotta get going. I have practice early tomorrow."

Shannon looks around. "But what about all the mess? We haven't finished cleaning up."

I'm relieved she's not going to fight me. "I'll come back with a crew on Sunday and get it done. You're off the hook."

Disappointment shadows her face. Because she can't talk to the ghost? Or because she likes spending time with me?

I'll probably never know. What does it matter anyway? A guy like me and a girl like Shannon—it wouldn't fly.

Look at these stupid thoughts. I'd never even be thinking them if we weren't in such a crazy situation. But adrenaline does crazy things to your brain.

Like making you think that the girl with the purple hair is actually kind of cool.

"Hurry up," I say gruffly.

Shannon's buttoning her coat. "Okay, okay," she says. "I gotta pee first, though, before we leave." Then her eyes get that little excited shimmer again. "And then on the way home, I'll tell you who I think we were talking to!"

I grunt and point to one of the kerosene lanterns. "Take that with you. And don't go far," I say, as she stoops to pick up a lantern.

"'Kay, Dad." She grins. She wraps her scarf around her neck and tucks the ends into her coat. "Be right back. Don't lock me out."

"It's tempting."

"Pff." She unhooks the door and pushes it open. A gust of wind snatches it from her hand and throws it wide, slamming it against the wall. My heart splurts into my throat and sticks there, pounding.

"Jesus Christ!" she yells. "What's with the wind?" She steps down, leaving the door open behind her. I prop it open with the brick—firmly this time, no way I'm closing myself in with some dead thing—and turn back inside.

I blow out two of the three remaining lanterns. As I cross the floor to blow out the third, my foot slips on the Ouija board. Better put that away.

I stoop to pick up the lid from where it sits on top of the board. It's still warm when my fingers touch it. Creepy.

The lid's still on GOODBYE.

I grab it. "Yeah, goodbye. Nice talking to you."

The lid skids across the board.

NO.

I give off a little squeak and pull my hand back.

Except it won't come. It's stuck.

My hand is damn well stuck on the cap.

I mean, really?

That's almost the worst part. Except it's not.

The worst part might even be when the lid starts moving over the letters, from one to the next to the next to the next while I watch, powerless to take my hand away. You'd think that was the worst. Except it's not.

The absolute worst part is when the boathouse door swings shut. Quietly. Just a little creak.

And when I look up.

And see the little hook dropping into the eye.

All by itself.

Chapter Ten

I stare at the door. The door that closed
all by itself.

Moved the brick.

Closed.

And locked itself.

My head spins. I feel like I might puke.

Under my fingers, the lid moves.
I try to pull away, but it won't let me. I go
to stand, but it's like my legs have been

cast in concrete. I'm stuck in this squat. My fingers are stuck to the lid.

I feel a sudden flash of heat, and my back breaks out in a sweat. Fear.

I try to push the lid off with my other hand. No dice. Those fingers become trapped too. Gorilla glue.

Now that both of my hands are on, the lid moves faster. With more purpose. My heart thrums as I watch—I can't tear my eyes away. I've heard that Ouija boards make a lot of spelling mistakes.

This one's not making any mistakes at all.

It's spelling out the same letters. Same order.

One name.

Over. And over. And over.

I nearly jump out of my shorts when something bangs on the door. Shannon.

"Elliot!" she yells. "Open up!"

Bangbangbang.

I try to stand, but the concrete's still holding me down. "Hang on!" I yell. I pull, but my hands are stuck. To the lid, which is stuck to the board. I'd pull it off the floor if I could, but it's stuck there too.

I fight a sudden urge to giggle.

"Open the door!" Shannon yells again. "I told you not to lock me out! It's freezing out here!"

I look at the door. The hook-and-eye closure tightens and loosens in time with Shannon's frantic tugging on the other side.

"Elliot! Please!"

I look back at the board, suddenly angry.

"What do you want?" I hiss. "What do you want from me?"

The lid heats up under my fingers, superhot. Agonizing. The heat travels up through my fingers and across my wrists.

It's like having hot wax shot through my veins.

"Ahhh!" I scream.

Shannon stops pounding. "Elliot?" Silence. "What's going on? Are you okay?"

The heat fades as quickly as it came. I'm left sweating, panting, my hands throbbing.

"I don't know what you want, you goddamn freak spirit."

The door starts rattling again as Shannon yanks and pounds on it. "Elliot, open the door!" she shrieks. "This isn't funny!" I can hear the fear in her voice. It feeds mine.

I open my mouth to tell her I can't. Before I can speak, the heat flares again. Up through my forearms and into my shoulders this time.

"Aaaaaaauuugh!" Pain descends on me like a red haze. The noises blur together.

Me screaming. Shannon screaming. Shannon pounding on the door with both fists, then kicking it with her boots.

"What do you want, Jessica?" I scream. That last bit, the name. I didn't know I was going to say it. It was pulled up from inside me. Thrown out of my mouth. By something other than me.

And just like snapping your fingers, all the craziness stops. The board releases me. I lurch sideways and fall over, hitting my head against a shelf.

There's a little metal plinking noise, and the door swings open. Shannon's standing there holding a brick, like she's about to plow it into the door. The lantern burns on the ground beside her, casting her face in an eerie underlight.

"What the hell is going on in here?" she bellows.

She looks at the door, then at me, lying on the floor.

She drops the brick and steps into the boathouse. I sit up and lean against a post, rubbing my head.

"What happened?" she demands.

"I'm okay," I say. "Thanks for asking. Can we leave now?"

She ignores my question. "Why were you screaming?" Her eyes fall on the Ouija board on the floor beside me. They narrow. She looks back at me. "You didn't."

"I couldn't help it."

"Bullshit!" she shouts. "I told you not to touch the board, Elliot! And you went ahead and did it by yourself!"

"I didn't do it on purpose!" I shout back. "It wouldn't let me go!"

Shannon tilts her head. "Oh, sure." She nods. "The Ouija board just reached up and grabbed you."

I shake my head. "No. Well, yeah, it did. I tried to move it out of the way so I could get by, and my fingers got stuck on the lid and it wouldn't let me go."

"Right. And you were powerless to pull away."

"I was," I say angrily. "It was like it was burning me." I point toward the door. "You heard me. You think I was making that up?"

She stares at me, trying to decide whether to believe me. "Why'd you lock me out?"

"I didn't."

"You goddamn well did, Elliot," she says, her voice rising.

"I didn't," I say. I haul myself to my feet with the help of a nearby shelf. "I didn't even touch the door. I propped it open with the brick when you left!"

Shannon looks like she's about to hit me.

"I didn't lock it," I insist. "I was sitting right there," I say, pointing to the floor. "I couldn't get up. The board wouldn't let me. The lid was moving and spelling out letters, and the door just...closed."

I shudder. "It locked by itself." Even as I say the words, I know how crazy they sound.

Shannon's eying me warily. "That's crap," she says. But the anger is gone from her voice. "Doors don't close and lock by themselves."

I raise my eyebrows in the direction of the door. "This one did. I watched it."

"That's impossible." She folds her arms and stares at me. "That stuff only happens in movies."

A movement at our feet catches our attention.

From where it came to rest after releasing my fingers, the lid stands up.

Stands right up.

On its side, slowly.

If my hair wasn't already curly, it sure as hell would be now.

As we watch, the cap starts to spin. Slow revolutions at first. It spins faster and faster until it's nothing but a white blur.

It stays precisely, impossibly, in one place.

"Yeah?" I say. I look at Shannon. "What movie would you say we're in?"

The blood drains from her face. Her hand creeps up to cover her mouth.

This party isn't over yet.

I ignore the crawling feeling inside my lower abdomen as I look down at the Ouija board. The cap's still spinning, hovering over just one word.

HELLO.

Chapter Eleven

"Did you say goodbye?" Shannon whispers. She can't tear her eyes from the board.

"No," I say. "I didn't say anything. I was just trying to put it away."

"What did it say?"

I don't answer. The last time that name hit the air…it wasn't me saying it.

"What did it say, Elliot?"

My head jerks up like I've been hit.

"Jessica." As I say it, the hairs on the back of my neck stand up. I feel sick. I want that cap to stop spinning.

I hear Shannon's sharp intake of breath. "What do you know about her?" she asks.

"Who, Jessica?"

"Yeah."

I shake my head. "I don't know anybody with that name."

"Oh my god," she whispers. Shannon's looking at me like maybe I'm going to sprout horns and a pitchfork. "This is real," she says. "This really is real. It really is."

I'm about to ask her who the hell this Jessica is, but then, without warning, she stomps on the spinning lid, smashing it flat with her heavy boot.

SLAM!

I jump about three feet. "What the hell?" I yell.

She winds up and kicks the Ouija board. It skitters away, under a wide shelf. It hits the wall with a thump. The lid spins out and comes to rest under a rack of life jackets.

"Act of god?" she says.

Then she starts to laugh. Big weird belly laughs.

I take it as a sign it's time to leave.

I grab Shannon's arm. "Okay," I say. I keep my voice calm. "You know what? We need to get out of here."

She stops laughing and stares at me for a second. Green eyes. Orange stripe in the left one.

I read the fear in them.

"Okay," she says.

But then the hysteria bubbles up again. I can see her trying to clamp down on it, but the laughter squeals out between her lips like air from a whoopee cushion.

Damn. She's freaking out.

I grab both of her arms then, just above her elbows. Crank her body around to face me.

"Shannon. We're leaving. Now." I give her a hard shake to bring her back down to Earth. "Get your things together."

She stops laughing. A shudder passes through her.

"But she's dead, Elliot," Shannon says. She seems dazed. "Don't you see? If Jessica's here, talking to us through a Ouija board, that means she's dead. She didn't just run away. Now we know for sure that Troy killed her."

"Who's Troy?" I cut her off before she can answer. "Never mind. Tell me later." Once we're headed home. As fast as my gas-guzzling 1988 Volvo station wagon will take us.

I steer her toward the door.

A new thought occurs to Shannon. She pulls her arm out of my grasp. "Oh my god, though, what if it maybe wasn't Troy? What if she was abducted and, like, held hostage by some creepy man? Like those stories you hear about girls who are stolen and then kept in some guy's backyard shed for decades before they escape? But maybe he got mad at her because she tried to escape and he killed her by accident?"

Shannon's voice is rising. I want to tell her to calm down, but I'm afraid it might make things even worse. Sometimes that happens with girls.

I also really want to know what the hell she's talking about. But not now. Right now, we've got only one job to do—and that's to get our asses out of here.

"But no, that can't be," Shannon's saying now. "She couldn't have been abducted and held hostage all summer, because she said she died in June."

I grab hold of her arm again. "I want to hear all your ideas. But once we're in the car, okay?" I pull. "We're leaving now."

"Okay. Right. Let's go." She nods, then looks at me. "But if she's dead, then what happened to her body?"

"Shannon."

"Okay, okay, I'm coming," she says. "But who's going to believe us about all this?"

God, the girl's brain is like a butterfly on Red Bull. I can't keep up.

We leave the board under the shelf—let someone else find it and wonder—and go to grab our bags. I sling mine over my shoulder and push open the door. I turn and hold it for Shannon.

"Hang on," she says.

"Come on, woman."

"And, but—wait," Shannon says. She cocks her head. "Why is she here, in the boathouse of all places?"

Now that we're leaving, her fear has taken a backseat to the excitement of solving a mystery. She's got a headful of theories.

And I'm sure she's going to fill mine with them on the way home.

Not an entirely bad way to pass the time, I think.

She bends to gather the lip gloss and books back into her bag.

That's when the door slams on my hand.

Chapter Twelve

The world combusts in a blistering explosion of agony.

I scream.

All this screaming. It's like we're part of some sort of psychotic carnival attraction. Come one, come all! Come hear what it sounds like when two dumb teenagers set an angry spirit free with a Ouija board!

My fingers are a rage of pain, and I'm pulling on them, yanking on them, but they're clamped tight between the frame and the door.

In my mind, I see those weekend warrior guys who go into the wilderness and get trapped between rocks and shit and end up having to saw their own limbs off.

No. I can't think about that right now.

Shannon turns to see what all the hollering's about. I see, rather than hear, her gasp.

"Oh my god, Elliot!"

She takes a step toward me, letting her bag drop. A pen bounces out. The books clatter back to the wooden floor. The yearbook falls open. Sunny faces smile up at me.

Suddenly the door loosens. I snatch my fingers back and stumble away from it. I grab my fingers with my other hand.

The pain is indescribable. I fold myself forward, holding both hands between my knees.

Dimly, I can hear yelling.

I'm pretty sure it's me.

I run out of breath. Right in that tiny pause where I'm deciding whether to scream again or just moan a little or maybe even sit right down and have a good old-fashioned cry, something in the boathouse changes.

The air. The pressure. It's like we've been shot up into the jet stream. All the way up to 30,000 feet, instant plane ride, with no time to adjust. My eardrums bow under the pressure.

Shannon smacks her hands over her ears.

The walls creak and groan. The floor squeals. Like nails being pulled up. There's a snapping sound from the beams above our heads.

The boathouse is taking a breath.

It feels like everything is sucking in—then a sudden wind blows outward from the center of the building. The floor cracks like thunder, and the whole place shakes like there's an earthquake below our feet. I grab for a pillar. The hangers holding the PFDS shimmy on the metal racks. The shades on the hurricane lanterns rattle.

What the—?

And then the whispering starts. It's like we're suddenly surrounded by twenty people. More. Dozens. Invisible people. Angry people, whispering loudly, all shushings and chatterings and hysterical, muffled shrieks.

Across the room, Shannon's hands are still covering her ears. But her face tells me she can hear the whispering too.

One word. Repeated over and over.

Listen.

Listen? To what? To whatever schizo ghost is living in this possessed shitshack?

The same one that just broke all my fingers?

No thanks.

But I'm not so sure I have a choice. I can feel the voices inside my head. There's no other way to explain it. They're chewing at my brain.

I can't deal with this.

"Stop," I whisper.

Nothing.

"Stop." Louder.

"Stop!" I yell it this time.

A piercing spike of white pain drives itself through my eye sockets. I fall to my knees, clutching my head. Shannon screams.

"Aauughh! No!" I shout.

In a flash, I see the little boy from *The Sixth Sense*. He's looking across his bedroom, at the tent that's got a little hump in it. The tent he just ran away from. He bolted when the ghost of that little girl showed up and puked on herself.

He stands there, watching the hump, terrified. She's waiting for him.

He doesn't want to see her.

But he has to. Because he knows what'll make her go away. He has to give her what she wants.

All she wants is to be heard.

He swallows his fear. Crosses his bedroom floor. Climbs back inside the tent. Sits down in front of the dead, barfing little girl.

And says, "Do you want to tell me something?"

All of a sudden, I get it. The whispering.

I get it.

Listen.

Do you want to tell me something?

"Okay," I say, quietly at first. "I hear you. I get it. You can quit now." The pain in my head intensifies, matching the agony in my fingers.

I crumple forward onto the floor. I wonder how much more I can take before I pass out.

"Elliot!" Shannon screams. "Elliot!" She scrambles over to my side and puts her hands on my shoulders, like she's trying to wake me from a bad dream.

"I get it!" I say. I'm almost sobbing now, the pain is so intense. My hands. My head. Shannon's screaming reaches me through the blur of voices clawing the insides of my mind. "You want me to listen," I say. "You just want to be listened to."

The pain ebbs, pulling away quickly like the tide sucking water from the rocks. But not enough.

I moan.

Shannon's draped over my back, hugging me and pulling on me and sobbing, and I'm kneeling on the floor, hanging on to my head with my busted fingers screaming, talking nonsense to an invisible thing that's tearing my brain apart.

The poor girl's going to lose her mind.

I might beat her to it.

"Jessica. It's Jessica, right?" I say. "I know you're here. I hear you. What do you want? I'll listen. I WILL LISTEN! Okay? Just—stop."

And just like that, everything stops. The pain, the whispering, everything.

It surprises me.

It's so quiet after all that noise.

I let out a ragged breath. Shannon sits back, but she keeps a hand on me. Slowly, I lower my hands.

My head feels fine. Clear and painless.

I sit up and flex my fingers, looking from one hand to the other. They feel fine too.

No blood.

No breaks.

No biggie.

I look at Shannon in wonder.

"Are you okay?" she says.

"I'm not sure if okay's the word," I say. "But my fingers are fine."

Shannon lets out a long breath.

I look at her. "That was scary."

Shannon's wide eyes follow my gaze toward the door. She runs her hands through her hair. "That was Amityville scary."

"Amityville?"

"Yeah. Didn't you ever watch *The Amityville Horror*?"

"No. Do I want to?"

"Probably not, after today."

We're quiet for a few seconds. "Act of god?" I ask.

She gives a weak laugh. "Well, I hope to hell that wasn't karma."

She looks at me. She tries to smile, but her lower lip trembles. When she speaks, her voice is only a whisper. "Are we going to get out of here, Elliot?"

Chapter Thirteen

This is bad.

We're trapped in an old boathouse on a Friday night with a ghost that's as pissed as a bull whose balls have just been burned off.

But I think I've got it figured out.

"We are going to get out of here," I tell Shannon.

I can tell she doesn't believe me.

"Right," she says, gesturing toward the door. "Like we can just open the door and walk out." She stands and walks to the door. Pushes on it. It won't budge.

"See?" she says. "So easy. Look! I'm outside already!"

She braces both arms against it and shoves.

"Shannon," I say, my voice a warning.

She ignores me. Pounds on the door with her fist. Kicks at it. Slams her shoulder into it.

Nothing. Which is probably good, because this is usually around the time all the weird stuff starts to happen. This ghost doesn't want us to leave, and any movement we make in that direction seems to rile it up.

Shannon points at the hook, which is dangling down, clearly not locking us in. "You think we'll get out?" she asks. "How do you figure? You just saw for yourself how easy it is to leave, Elliot."

I can hear the tears in her voice. "We're trapped in here."

"We are not trapped," I say. Maybe it's a lie. But the words make me feel better.

Shannon leans her head against the door. I hear her sniff. "I don't want this to be happening," she whispers.

"Well, we're in it now," I say. "Not much we can do except to give this... Jessica...what she wants."

"Which is?"

"To be heard. She seems to have something to say."

Shannon snorts. "I'll say."

"Why don't you spare me all the mystery, Shannon, and tell me who she is?"

After a moment, Shannon lifts her head. She turns and slides down the door until her butt's resting on the floor. She leans her elbows on her knees and sighs. "She was a senior," she says. "Jessica Chapman. She was pretty. Beautiful.

Ridiculous, really. Captain of the cheer-leading team. She disappeared after a football game last spring. Just vanished. It made the news and everything. They had a manhunt going for days. They couldn't find any trace of her." She shivers.

News to me. I don't read the paper or listen to the radio.

"I haven't heard anything about it," I say. Even though I'm new to Wildwood, surely people are still talking about a missing person?

She shakes her head. "I haven't heard much, either, since school started up," she says. "Maybe we talked it all out in June. And I guess life goes on. She was two grades ahead of me anyway."

"What do they think happened?"

Shannon shrugs. "Some people said she ran away," she says. "Too much pressure at home, too much pressure at school. She was the best at, like, everything. Good marks, lots of friends. She was expected to flatten everyone at the regional cheerleading championships, like she did the year before," Shannon says. "But she never got the chance."

"Why not?"

"She disappeared a week before the competition." Shannon shrugs. "Maybe she just...took off. Maybe it was too hard to be such a perfect person."

Hear that. I could've had a whole big conversation with Jessica about it.

"A lot of other people, though, they think her boyfriend killed her," Shannon says.

"This Troy guy?"

She nods. "Troy Joliette, yeah. He didn't even go to grad because that's all anyone was talking about."

"They have anything on him?"

"I didn't follow it all that closely," Shannon admits. "He went away to college this fall. I think he's still a suspect though."

"Why do people think he did it?"

She shakes her head. "I don't think anyone thinks there's any good reason, really. Troy and Jessica were totally in love."

I wouldn't be so sure. I think about what my mom says. How you never know from the outside what people's relationships are like on the inside. It explains a lot about her and my dad, she told me. How everyone thought they had it all together until one day they just...didn't.

"Maybe they weren't as in love as everybody thought," I say.

Shannon looks doubtful. "Maybe not. But even if they weren't that in love, I still can't see it," she says. "Troy was a really nice guy."

I think about how I felt about Shannon before I spent any time with her. The assumptions I made.

"Appearances can be deceiving," I say.

She nods. "For sure, they can."

"Let me guess," I say. "This Troy. He was the captain of the football team."

Shannon looks at me in shock. "How did you know?"

"Captain of the football team dating the captain of the cheerleading team?" I laugh. "It's the American Dream, baby."

She raises her eyebrows at me. "Yeah, but in the American Dream, your boyfriend's not supposed to kill you."

That's when the lightbulb above us shatters.

Chapter Fourteen

I duck and cover. Shannon shrieks.

What did we say that made the light explode? The American Dream thing? Or was it the thing about her boyfriend killing her?

Listen.

I'm all ears, I think.

Now that there's just the one lantern

going in here, it feels downright scary. What if it goes out?

I glance around for the other ones. Maybe I'll light them back up.

A noise from under a shelf makes my skin crawl. The Ouija board slides into view. It creeps toward us, scraping across the tiny grains of dirt strewn on the wooden floor. *Ssshhkiff.*

My brain goes all swimmy for a few seconds.

Shannon makes a tiny noise deep in her throat. She pulls her legs in tight to her chest.

The board stops half a foot away from me.

And how is it that the chalk hasn't even started to fade?

"I think she wants to talk," I say.

"I'm not so sure I want to talk," Shannon says.

When the lid rolls toward me— on its edge, like a hula hoop that a small child might roll down a country lane, the most normal thing in the world— Shannon takes a shaky breath.

"I'm not so sure we have much choice," I say.

We watch as the lid settles itself on the board.

HELLO.

Adrenaline shoots into my lower gut. I think about the last time I touched that thing. The burning.

Then I think about the door slamming on my fingers.

And the pain in my head.

Listen.

We really have no choice.

I reach out and pull the board toward me, ignoring the fear that flares in my belly.

I put my fingers on the lid.

Let's get this show on the road.

I look at Shannon. She's biting her lip. Thinking.

Then she puts her hands on. We lock eyes across the board, a couple of soldiers about to jump into combat without knowing whether our chutes will open.

I'll do the talking this time.

The lone lantern flickers as I turn my attention to the board. "Are we speaking with Jessica?"

A shiver arcs up my spine as the lid moves. Without hesitation it slides to YES.

"How did you die, Jessica?"

My scalp tightens as the letters are spelled out.

R-O-P-E.

My eyes skip away from the board, toward the coils of ropes hanging from large hooks on the wall.

I look back at the board. "Were you strangled, Jessica?"

YES.

Shannon swallows and closes her eyes.

"Did you die here, Jessica? In this boathouse?" We've already asked her whether she's ever been in here, and she said no. But maybe she was wrong. Or lying. Because why else would she be here?

NO.

A ripple of relief floods me. Somehow it's better to imagine that she didn't actually die inside this place. But then, if not here...where?

"Where did you die?"

D-O-C-K.

The same dock that's just outside the door.

Shannon makes a thin noise.

"Where are you now, Jessica?" I ask. "Where is your body?"

No answer.

"Was she strangled and dumped?" Shannon asks. "What kind of boyfriend would do such a thing?"

"If she was dumped," I say, "then her body must still be in the lake."

"That's, like, all around us," Shannon whispers. "She could be anywhere. She could be right under us, Elliot." She peeks down between her knees, like she can see into the water below.

"Did Troy Joliette kill you?" I ask. Better get our facts straight.

The lid flies to NO so fast, my fingers almost slide off.

We exchange glances.

"Not Troy?" Shannon says.

Like a slapshot, the yearbook slides across the floor.

Shannon screams. I can't blame her. We should expect the unexpected by now, but I guess there's still room for surprises.

I jerk my leg away from where the book hits me. "Jesus."

We watch as the pages begin to turn, riffling forward, then backward. When they finally settle, we're looking at a two-page photographic spread of the Wildwood Cheer Team.

I sit back and take my hands off the board.

Shannon's attention pivots back to me. "Don't take your hands off!"

I shoot her a look of exasperation. "Or what? Or I'll let the spirit out? Bit late for that."

She stares at me. Then, with an irritated little huff, she takes her hands off too. We look at the yearbook.

"I don't like this," I say.

She snorts. "Have you liked any of this?"

I'm already edgy. I don't want to be here any more than she does.

And I didn't even get us into this mess.

I look straight at her. "It was going okay until you had your dumb idea to make a Ouija board."

She stares at me. "You're blaming me for this?"

I look around. "Uh, who else is there? It wasn't my idea."

Shannon presses her lips together. When she speaks, her voice is tight. "Well, I'm not the genius who touched the Ouija board when he wasn't supposed to," she says.

Something inside me snaps. "It wasn't my fault, Shannon," I roar.

She recoils like I've slapped her.

A cold wind pushes its way up through the cracks in the boathouse floor. The roof creaks. I look up to see dust spilling from a hole in the ceiling.

Shannon looks up too. "Can't this just be over?"

Then she bursts into tears.

Chapter Fifteen

Oh god. I feel awful. I shouted at her and made her cry.

Like we don't already have enough to deal with.

I can't stand the sight of Shannon with her hands over her face like this. I shuffle closer and put my arm over her shoulders.

She lets herself lean against me. I pull her into a hug, wrapping my arms around her. She melts into my chest and tucks her head under my chin and cries and cries.

Her hair smells like watermelons.

After a while her sobs ebb into sniffles, but she's shivering. We sit like that for I don't know how long. Until she stops crying, I guess.

Shannon wipes her eyes with the backs of her hands, leaving behind dark streaks from her makeup. She gives a quavery laugh.

"That was weird," she says. She's still leaning against my chest.

"What? That wind under the floor?"

"No, the crying. Well, yeah, the wind too." She takes a shuddery breath. "I haven't bawled like that since I was maybe ten."

I give her a little squeeze. "Fear'll do that to you."

She looks up at me. Her eyes are pretty in the lamplight. Her lashes are still wet.

Cat's eyes.

"I guess," she says. She gives me a little half smile.

And before I even think about what I'm doing, I'm kissing her. I feel her gasp of surprise, but she's right there to meet me, her hands twining up around and behind my neck. Her mouth feels like velvet.

We pull away and look at each other, shocked. She stares at me, wide-eyed, her hand covering her mouth, like we've just done something outrageous.

What am I doing?

More.

Shannon reaches for me, and I pull her close, sliding my hands into her hair. She presses herself against me. I feel the blood rushing into every part of my body. Hot. Dizzy. Her mouth opens under mine, and I imagine how the hard steel of her piercing will feel against my tongue. I taste her breath against my lip—

My phone beeps.

Shannon and I fly apart. We stare at each other, terror mixed in with something new.

With shaking hands, I pull my phone out of my pocket and look at the display. If it says anything crazy like Jessica, I know I'm headed for permanent residency in the insane asylum.

Assuming I get out of here, that is.

No ghost. It's just some random telemarketer. They're always calling around dinnertime.

But sitting there, staring at the phone in my hand, I have an idea. How did I not think of it before?

I look at Shannon, and right there, I see it in her eyes too. She nods, silent. Excited.

I'm going to call someone and get us hauled out of here.

I raise my thumb to key in my password. But then I stop.

My mind flashes back to having my fingers slammed in the door.

The burning.

The hot pokers in my eye sockets.

I take a long, slow breath in.

The air in the boathouse has gone unnaturally still. It's utterly, deafeningly silent.

Everyone's waiting.

On me.

I'm feeling torn. I want to call, but I'm terrified of what might happen. So really, there's only one reasonable decision to make.

Only one decision that guarantees no one gets hurt.

I exhale slowly. I reach forward—slow-mo—and place my phone on the floor in front of me. Moving carefully, I push it away so it's out of reach.

I feel Shannon sag against my chest a bit when I put the phone down, but I think she understands. Disaster averted.

The phone grazes the yearbook, which is still sitting open on the floor beside us. Still open to the page full of chirpy cheerleaders.

I pull the lantern toward the pages and lean in for a closer look.

"Which one is Jessica?" I run my finger along the list of names under the photo, looking for a J.

Shannon points at a girl sitting in the center of the group. Front row, seated on a low bench. She balances a huge trophy on her lap. Big grin.

Shannon was right. She's a babe.

"What's the trophy for?" I ask.

"The Laurel Cup," she says. "It's given to the top cheerleading squad. It went to Wildwood last year."

"And Jessica's holding it because she's the captain?"

"Well, the team won because of her," Shannon says.

I look at the girls. Their happy, smiling faces. Eerie to think that one of them is now dead.

My eyes skip down to Jessica again. Specifically, that one.

"Hey," I say, leaning closer. "Is that like the necklace you found in the bin?"

"Where?"

"Right there." I point to a girl sitting beside Jessica in the photograph. Her hair is tied back, the end of her ponytail curled loosely beside her open collar. She isn't laughing like the others. Instead, her smile looks tight.

Shannon peers at the picture.

"Yeah, it's the same one. The BEST. Weird." Her mouth drops open. "Oh my god," she breathes.

When her eyes meet mine, there's a sudden understanding in them.

"That's Sam Stokes."

I'm drawing a blank.

"Sam Stokes?" I ask. "Who's she?"

Shannon releases a long breath. "She's Jessica's best friend. Or she was. Or at least I thought she was."

I look back at the photograph. Slowly, things begin to slide into place.

"So…" I say. "Sam's got one half of the necklace. And…"

"Jessica would have had the other half," Shannon finishes.

We both look to see whether the matching half is around Jessica's neck. But you can't see her neck because of the Laurel Cup.

"The cup's in the way," I say. "So we have no way of knowing whether she had the other half or not."

Shannon looks at me. "Yes, we do."

Chapter Sixteen

We sit facing each other. Shannon pulls the board over and arranges it between us. The chalk looks just as clear as it did when Shannon printed all the letters out.

That seems like a week ago.

"Did you have the other half of that necklace, Jessica?" she asks.

YES.

My scalp crawls.

I look up at Shannon. "Which bin did you find the necklace in?"

She turns and points. "That one." Then she shakes her head. "But it's not there anymore," she says.

"Where is it?" I ask.

"I dropped it, remember? When the door slammed that first time?"

"Right." I do remember. I scan the floor for the little silver chain. I hope it didn't fall through the floorboards. Because the boathouse is right on the dock. And the dock is right over the water.

I don't see it.

Damn.

"Oh, but...oh my god," Shannon says. Her eyes widen, and she scrambles to her feet. "In that bin. There was rope in that bin, Elliot. Lots of it. The thin kind."

"Rope?" I look at her. "Aren't we looking for a necklace?"

Suddenly I get it.

Thin rope. The perfect kind of rope to wrap around someone's neck.

The necklace, found in a bin full of exactly that kind of rope.

But how likely is it—how perfect—that the suspected killer would actually have her necklace come undone at exactly the right moment, leaving it behind in a bin full of potential murder weapons?

Unless…

I grab Shannon's hand and pull her back down to the floor with me.

I put my fingers on the lid. "Did Sam strangle you with the rope that's in the bin?"

YES.

Shannon shudders.

"Did you fight her?"

YES.

I glance up at Shannon. She nods.

"Why did Sam strangle you?"

The lid moves like it's going somewhere, but then it just sort of stops.

Shannon takes her hands off and looks at me. "What kind of question is that?"

"What?" I ask.

"It's too open-ended," she says. "Everything has to be spelled out. That could be, like, eight paragraphs."

"So? It's not like we're in any sort of hurry."

"But we don't really need Jessica to explain it all. It's already pretty obvious why Sam would want to see Jessica dead."

"What? Why?"

Shannon rolls her eyes. "You are such a guy."

"That's a bad thing?"

She sighs. "I think Sam was completely jealous of Jessica," she says. "She had the looks, the boyfriend, the marks, the talent." Shannon glances down at the photo in the yearbook. "The cheerleading cup," she adds.

"But they were best friends," I say. "I don't get it."

"They probably were, for a while," Shannon says. "Maybe even for a long time. Those necklaces? They probably had those since they were little. That's the kind of thing young girls wear."

I nod toward the board. "Ask her."

"And over time," Shannon says, finishing her thought, "as Jessica got more and more successful, I'll bet Sam started to hate her guts." She moves to put her hands on the board.

The second she touches it, the lid flies to YES.

A chill slips through me.

Sick. A best friend who turns into a jealous killer?

"And, oh my god, I get it now," says Shannon. Her eyes widen as she looks at me. "Jessica disappeared the week before the cheerleading finals."

"Right, so?"

"Sam won, Elliot. She took the championship for Wildwood."

I give a low whistle. "She didn't want any competition for the cup. And Jessica was just too tough to beat."

Shannon turns back to the board. Her next question is interrupted by a soft grating noise. We turn our heads to see a necklace appearing from between two floorboards. The tiny silver links roll up and over the edge of one board, coiling up like rope on a ship's deck.

My skin breaks out in goose bumps.

We watch until it's finished moving.

Shannon shivers and looks at me.

"And there's your evidence," I say. I push myself to my feet and walk to the spot where the necklace sits, bunched up on the boards.

"Which one is it?" Shannon asks.

I squat down to examine it, but I can't see a thing. I bring the lamp over.

"It's the BEST. Same one as before."

"Sam's part," Shannon says.

"So then where's the other half?" I ask.

We look at each other, and then Shannon looks back at the board. "Jessica, were you wearing part of this necklace when you died?"

YES.

Shannon swallows. "Where are you now?"

With a low squeak, the door swings open.

Chapter Seventeen

We shiver as the evening air rushes in.

I'm not sure if it's because it's cold or dark or just plain freaky out there, but I'm not in any rush to leave the boat-house, even after all our wishing that we could leave. It's funny.

Or almost funny.

I turn to Shannon. "Shall we?"

She nods and gets to her feet. I blow out the lantern and set it on the shelf beside the padlock.

The breeze from the lake is sharp. Shannon wraps her scarf around her neck and slips her mittens on. I zip my hoodie.

"We still don't know how Sam's necklace came off," I say. As we step out of the boathouse and onto the dock, I feel lighter somehow. I don't feel like any weird things are going to happen now. Jessica's story has been told. She doesn't need to slam any more doors or move stuff around or burn people to get them to pay attention to the truth.

To listen.

"Jessica said she fought against Sam," Shannon says. "The necklace could easily have come loose in a struggle."

I think about that for a minute. "Man, that'd be a hell of a fight."

Shannon nods. "You don't want to mess with someone who's strong enough to lift another human being into the air while shaking a pom-pom and spelling out W-I-L-D-C-A-T-S."

"Especially if she's mad," I say.

"But there's not much you can do if someone sneaks up on you and throws a rope around your neck."

My words settle over us. We go quiet for a few minutes as we look out at the lake. The wind's calmed down now. The night is almost still.

"There," Shannon says. She points down the dock a little ways, off to one side. I look, but I can't see anything.

She crosses the distance in a few quick steps and kneels down, hanging on to the edge with her mittened hands.

"Oh my god, she's here," Shannon says. Her voice is thick with tears.

I follow, peering into the depths. Is she seeing a light or something?

I strain my eyes against the dark, but I can't see anything.

Shannon's crying now, sniffling and wiping her nose and sitting right near the edge of the dock with her legs all bundled up against her body. I sit beside her.

"How do you know she's here?" I ask.

She takes a deep breath and releases it slowly. "I can feel her," she says. "You know? Can you feel her too?"

I close my eyes and try to feel, but all I can think about is how damn cold I am.

"She's free now," Shannon says.

I get that. I felt that release when I left the boathouse. So I guess I did feel Jessica, after all. On her way to a better place.

Shannon sniffs and glances back toward the boathouse. "But how did the necklace end up back in the bin?" she asks.

I suppress a laugh. Nothing can stop the relentless whirring and clicking in this girl's brain.

"Well, they would have fought on the dock, right?" she says. "And then the necklace would have fallen off into the water."

I shrug. "Maybe it came loose and only fell off later. Maybe when Sam was putting the lid back on the bin? Covering her tracks?"

Shannon nods. "Maybe." We sit there, huddled together on the dock, looking out across the dark lake. I slip my arm around her shoulders.

My touch triggers more questions.

"But, then," she asks, "how would Sam have even gotten into the boat-house in the first place? How would she have bypassed the padlock?"

"Well, when we got there today, it wasn't even locked," I tell her. "When I went to put the key in, the padlock was already open. So it could have been open this whole time, I guess."

Shannon looks at me. "But why was it unlocked? Who left it that way?"

I smile and touch her hair.

She smiles back. "Look at us," she says. "All sleuthing."

"Like we have any clue what really went down," I agree. Dozens of unanswered questions swirl around us.

She glances back toward the boathouse. "But who's going to believe us that we were talking to a ghost?"

"We leave the ghost part out of it," I say. "We just have to show them the necklace."

"And what, they'll automatically connect it to Jessica's disappearance?"

"The photo in the yearbook," I remind her. "That's a pretty clear connection to who owned the necklace. Finding Sam's necklace down here is reason enough for them to investigate."

Shannon looks back at the dark water in front of her.

"They'll find her," I say softly.

She nods, without words for once.

I stand and hold my hand out to her. She takes it, and I pull her up from the dock.

I can just imagine what Harrison's going to say to me once the police are involved. Something about sending me out to clean up and instead getting a dead body dumped in his lap.

I laugh.

"What?" she asks.

"Harrison."

"What about him?"

"Just what he's going to say about all this."

"Who gives a rip?" Shannon growls. For a second, I see a flash of the girl I thought she was before this whole thing started.

All two and a half hours ago.

Not too often your entire outlook on life changes in such a short span.

"You're right." I nod. "Karma'll take care of him."

"Or an act of god," she says. She laughs, and for a second I wonder what it's going to be like between us.

And then I catch her eye, and she presses herself against me and wraps my arm around her shoulders, holding it there.

And I know it's going to be great.

Alex Van Tol admits to having made more than one Ouija board in her lifetime, but has never, to her knowledge, unleashed any angry demons. She dreams up creepy plotlines in her seaside home of Victoria, British Columbia. Which, incidentally, she shares with a ghost. Visit her on the Interwebs at www.alexvantol.com.